The Troll's Belt

Also by J.M. Ney-Grimm

The Troll's Belt

by J.M. Ney-Grimm

Wild
Unicorn

ISBN-13: 978-0615896298
ISBN-10: 0615896294

Designed by JMNG

Cover photography:
"Wooden Window" by Anna Dudek / Dreamstime.com
"Fantasy Treehouse" by Catia Amadio / Dreamstime.com
"Boy Scowling" by E.J. White / Dreamstime.com

The Troll's Belt

For
Lucy Ann
&
Ben

Cosstrand

Silmaren

Erice

hathorlynd

Fiorish

Meerovessic Sea

Auberon
Pavelle

Cambers

Solmondy

Giralliya

Istria

Bazinthiad

The North-lands

$\mathcal{B}$rys slammed the door behind him and stomped across his room in fury.

It wasn't fair. It just wasn't fair.

Did Jol have to sweep the floors each afternoon when school let out?

No.

Did Jol have to wash the curing cheese wheels in his motter's dairy?

No.

Did Jol have to help put up vats of kraut when too many cabbages were ready in the garden?

Of course not.

It wasn't fair, it wasn't fair, it wasn't fair!

He banged open the shutters of his bed nook,

threw himself down on the mattress, and punched his pillows a few times.

And now he wouldn't get to go to the solstice bonfire either, shun it!

Lars' patter had promised that all the kids old enough could come early and build the fire. Lars said there would be rope-climbing contests, a juggling tournament, and limb-running races.

Shun it! Shun it! Shun it!

Why had he answered back when Patter reminded him of the sweeping chore? He knew it was his responsibility. It was just . . . that he'd thought he'd finished everything.

Pilka and Pehmea, their household reindeer, retrieved from today's herd boy, milked, and settled in the byre.

Cheeses washed, turned, and re-weighted.

Clean laundry fetched from Aunt Mersela and put away.

And the mended chair delivered to Froiken Ildsdotter.

Everything tidy, the chores complete, and his time his own. The schoolmaster had even refrained from setting homework in honor of the evening festival, so the rest of the day was his.

Except then Patter had returned unexpectedly from the mill – something about a caliper-and-chisel set forgotten and needed for one of the men – just as Brys was heading for the entry staircase.

Patter took one look around and said sternly, "Why is there still mud on this floor?"

And Brys had answered, "Because *you* tracked it in."

And that had been that: a nasty shouting match between them, culminating with Patter's decree that Brys spend the afternoon and evening in his room. Not fair!

He gave another punch to his pillows, but it was half-hearted.

I should have just bitten my tongue. Why didn't I?

It wasn't really about the sweeping. It was . . . that Patter seemed to think Brys was trying to skive off without finishing his chores on purpose. Why couldn't he assume the best, instead of the worst? Or have asked . . . something else?

Brys had just forgotten, that was all.

And this wasn't the only instance either. Patter seemed poised for criticism, pouncing on each small fault, convinced Brys wanted to do less than his fair share. And it just wasn't so.

He knew why – besides milking the reindeer, splitting firewood, weeding the garden, and repainting the house stilts with rendered pine sap – he had to do a bunch of other stuff too. Sweep, wash dishes, dust, put away clothes, help put up vegetables and all. It had been him and Patter alone for all his life.

Jol had his motter, Aunt Mersela, to pitch in on all the daily chores.

Now, it was true that Aunt Mersela was known to split firewood when her temper was up, so Jol had to wash dishes on those days. But they had three to do all that needed doing.

He and Patter had just themselves. And Patter did the mill accounts in the evenings at home.

How had Patter managed? Way back when?

Brys could remember that when he was very, very small, he'd spent days with Aunt Mersela and nights at home and hadn't *any* chores. In fact, he'd thought Aunt Mersela his motter (and called her so) until he went to school and learned otherwise.

But Patter must have done everything himself. No . . . maybe not.

They'd always eaten at Aunt Mersela's and Uncle Karl's table. He remembered that, now he came to think. Even after he started school, they walked across the garden between the two houses every morning for breakfast and every evening for supper. And Aunt Mersela had packed his and Patter's dinner pails. She still did their laundry.

So Patter hadn't had to worry about meals or cleaning up after them. Really he'd organized things pretty well. And Uncle Karl – Patter's younger brother – had been generous with help.

Why couldn't Patter understand now that Brys knew how things were? Knew he needed to pitch in? Knew he had to do his best? Why did Patter assume the worst?

Brys shrugged and slouched moodily over to the window.

He could see most of Glinhult straggling up the hamlet's hill to the clearing at its top surrounded by towering Wych elms. A few folk were still bustling around their homes – most stilt houses like his, a few the old-style tree eyries – putting away hoes and digging forks, locking the doors to the chicken coop, or carrying full milk buckets up to their kitchens. But they'd join the crowd on the hill soon.

I must be the only one who won't be there, he thought savagely.

Not fair! So not fair!

He dragged a low stool over and sat, resting his forearms on the window sill.

There were the Tirillsdotter sisters now securing the byre under their home – where Talja and Syoja were settling for the night – and strolling toward the hilltop. He saw Oskar and Pietur join them. Lars would already be there, undoubtedly arranging the scrap from the lumber mill along with household discards just so, to be sure the bonfire would burn well. Aunt Mersela and Uncle Karl had left early, declaring that if Jol got a holiday from chores (and they'd allowed him that), so did his elders.

A year ago, Patter would have done the same for Brys. Was it something about him turning twelve that had changed everything? But Jol was thirteen, and Uncle Karl was just the same.

Brys gritted his teeth.

Was that a flicker of flame on the hill? A spiral of smoke?

It was hard to tell. Dusk wouldn't arrive until long after the bonfire was started, the days of full summer being so long. He narrowed his eyes.

Yes!

The fire was well and truly started. It must have caught with the first few grinds on the tinder wheel. A good omen, that.

His shoulders sagged.

I'm not there, and I'm not going to be there.

He sighed. Then straightened.

Wait a moment . . . why not? Why not go despite Patter's prohibition?

Brys chewed his lip thoughtfully. So . . . disobey Patter? He generally didn't. But, *generally*, Patter was reasonable. Why seek trouble when it was unnecessary?

But *this* wasn't reasonable.

Miss the solstice fire just because he'd forgotten to sweep the floors?

I won't, he decided. *I don't care. I'm not going to mope here at the window all evening, while everyone else has fun.*

He jumped to his feet, almost knocking over the stool in his haste, crossed the room to the cupboard by his bed nook, and rummaged in its bottom drawer.

There it was: his winter cap.

He'd need to hide his hair, or Patter would spot him, even in the crowd, and Brys didn't intend to return home until he was good and ready. There were other redheads in Glinhult, but they were many years older or younger.

What else could he do to make sure Patter didn't see him and summarily enforce discipline?

I know! I'll borrow Jol's new tunic. He hasn't worn it yet, so Patter won't recognize it. And Jol won't mind. He'd suggest it, if he were here.

Plans settled, Brys hurried from his room, but cast a glance around the gathering area of the house. Yup, sink empty and clean. Table wiped and clear. Armchairs and settle free of jackets, book bags, and other debris.

He stepped around the bannister to the house entry and pulled up the trap door.

Sias shun it! Patter really had been mad, to close the trap in the month of Joiesse.

Brys hooked it open.

Their stairs down to the ground had been enclosed for as long as he could remember, and they used the trap door only in winter. Even then, if they were expecting guests, they left it open and lit the small tile stove beside the straight door to warm the stair hall.

This door he closed carefully behind him, then galloped through the flower and vegetable garden, in through his cousin's straight door, then up the stairs.

Their trap was open, secured to the wall with a hook, as usual.

He rounded the newel post, heading for the next flight of stairs.

Uncle Karl had built with a bigger family in mind, so Jol's room was one of two tucked under the roof. Brys had always envied his cousin the cozy feeling the slanting ceiling gave to the space and his cushioned window seat in the dormer niche. Its high view made Brys imagine himself a hawk in a tree top, surveying all of Glinhult from the sky.

Ignoring the window for now, he doffed his own tunic and pulled Jol's over his shirt. It was big. Jol had hit a growth spurt after his last name-day, gaining half a head on Brys and adding shoulder width as well. But the tunic wasn't impossible.

Brys lolloped down the stairs again, paused, then tiptoed into Aunt Mersela's bedroom to check himself in her mirror. Would his misdirection with hat and tunic be disguise enough?

Not if he let his jaw-length hair stick out below the hat.

Hmm. What to do, what to do?

He looked over Aunt Mersela's dressing table. Brys' hair wasn't long enough to tie in a horsetail the way Jol did his, but maybe two of his aunt's clips could fasten the front bits to the back of his head. It was only the front bits that were showing.

He wasn't used to hair clips and fumbled them in several too-loose attempts, before achieving something that seemed likely to stay put. He jumped while tossing his head. Nothing shook free.

Time to go!

He'd already missed the lighting, the hymn, and the blessing, but the best was yet to come. He scurried for the hilltop.

His cousin didn't recognize him for a moment, even when Brys came smash up to him.

Jol stared blankly, then laughed. "Brys! What are *you* doing here? Uncle Arn said you weren't coming." He paused, then protested, "Hey! That's my tunic, you thief! Give it back!" He punched Brys in the shoulder, but half-heartedly. Brys shoved him back with equal lack of enthusiasm.

"I needed it, Jol," he insisted. "And you weren't home to ask, now were you?"

Jol smirked. "Day off from chores," he reminded. "So what gives?"

"Patter rated me for not sweeping, and I gave him a flip back answer," Brys admitted.

Jol's jaw dropped a shade. "You back answered Uncle Arn?"

"Um, yeah."

"And you're here? With leave?" Jol closed his mouth, but his eyes widened.

"Without leave."

"Thus my tunic." Jol shook his head. "And your winter hat. Huh."

"Patter's been so grouchy. I can't do anything right," Brys burst out. "I decided I just wasn't going to knuckle under one more time."

"You *are* brave." Jol gave him a curious look, then grinned. "So are you going to sneak around the fringes or be bold and join the fun?"

"Some of each," Brys admitted.

"Are you up for the rope climbing? It's about to start!" Jol bounced on his heels.

"Who's judging?"

"Old Matts."

"He won't notice anything," Brys asserted. "He hardly sees well enough to greet me in the street at high noon. Come on! Let's go!"

He actually won second place in the rope

climbing, which triumph gave him courage to enter the limb racing.

Patter subbed in for Herr Olson as judge halfway through the heats, but seemed to notice nothing amiss with the contestant in the black hat and crisp, new clothing.

It was probably a good thing Brys came in seventh. Likely none of the runners were very visible as they raced along the branches high above the ground, dodging twigs and leaf clumps. But Brys doubted his disguise would have passed muster, if Patter had handed him one of the carved boomerangs being passed out as prizes.

The rest of the evening was equally satisfactory.

Playing tag as the shadows deepened. Watching the last round of the juggling contest where the winner lofted twenty-five balls into the air and kept them up in a flashing, elongated arc stretching as high as the flames of the bonfire. Scarfing down sweet nut pastries. And finally settling around the fire as it burned down to tell haunt stories and jokes or to just tip his head back to look at the stars.

I'm glad I came, he thought.

That was before he arrived home sometime after midnight.

Patter was sitting at the table, waiting, when Brys climbed the stairs and emerged through the trap.

For a moment, they simply looked at one another, Patter grim and angry, Brys with a sinking sensation in his stomach.

"So." Patter's voice was even, but held a disturbing undertone. "You chose to leave the house, when I bade you keep within it. No doubt your reason seemed good to you." His eyes were flat.

Brys swallowed, trying to recapture his bravado.

It eluded him, but a spark of his earlier indignation straightened his spine. He lifted his chin.

"You weren't fair. I'd made a mistake, and you were hoping for it."

"This isn't about sweeping the floor, Brys." Not even a hint of understanding warmed Patter's face, which stayed cold and implacable. "You disobeyed me. In a sneaky and underhanded way. In your actions, you lied. You broke the trust between us."

That internal spark struck tinder, and Brys was furious, although the chill in his middle still ate at his courage. How dare Patter speak so!

"You broke it first, shun you!"

"Enough!"

Patter rose to his feet, controlled, but with menace in his movement.

"You made pretense of obedience, then once my back was turned, you dropped an inconvenient loyalty and used disguise and my absence to flout me. How dare you accuse *me* of broken trust! How have *I* ever deceived you?"

Patter trod deliberately closer.

Brys stood his ground and swallowed, deeper anger thrusting apprehension aside.

"Never, shun you!" he spat. "You broke my trust when you started hunting up my mistakes, when you forgot that errors merit teaching and forgiveness, not punishment!"

Patter's hand came up. Brys struggled to stay put, not to flinch. He glared upward, refusing to cower.

With effort, Patter lowered his arm to his side.

"Go. To. Your. Room." His chest rose and fell as though he'd just felled a tree. "Now."

Brys glared a moment more, nodded jerkily, and turned on his heel. He carefully *didn't* slam his door.

On the other side of it, he leaned against its thick panels in shaken reaction.

Sias in Sanember!

He'd never seem Patter like that before. Was his forbidden participation in the solstice really so bad? He didn't think so, despite Patter's frigid fury. Some thing else must be wrong.

I am not the problem, he insisted to himself. *Something's changed, and Patter is . . . worried?*

What an odd conclusion to draw.

He shook his head, stooping to remove his shoes.

Patter might be worried – was worried, insisted his intuition – but dang if he knew why.

I'll observe him, Brys decided, *and see if I can't notice something. And* – he made another resolution – *I'll double check everything I do.* No mistakes on the morrow.

This decision allowed him to sleep, hoping the morning would be better.

It was, but not much.

Patter's rage had subsided into a false calm, marked by even courtesy and no warmth.

It was the sevenday, so no school awaited Brys. He milked Pehmea and Pilka, then took them to Diri, who had herd duty for the day. Then he mucked out the byre, washed his hands and saw to the cheeses, and picked a bushel of fresh greens.

He and Patter had intended to put up a cask of gundru, as well as starting a batch of kjaeldermelk, but Brys suspected their plans had changed. Hoped so. Working side by side with the distant stranger Patter had become would be worse punishment than missing a half-dozen festivals.

Patter met him at the trap, considerately took the bushel basket from him, and gestured at the table. "Go sit," he instructed.

Brys did as he was told, watching as Patter dumped the greens in the filled sink, swished them around to remove any sand and dirt clinging to the leaves, then ladled them into an oversized colander to drain. He check the vast kettle where the milk was heating, covered it, and removed it from the stove.

Then he joined Brys at the table, selecting the seat at Brys' right, rather than the one around the corner.

Brys turned his head warily and inched himself to the far edge of his seat.

What was Patter up to?

The gentleness with which he'd taken the bushel basket and his choice to sit side-by-side seemed to indicate forgiveness, even kindliness. But the lack of light in Patter's eyes, the sternness about his mouth, contradicted any such softening.

Brys didn't know what to expect.

Patter clasped his hands together on the table, simulating an ease belied by his hard voice.

"You're right," he began abruptly. "I've been harsh of late. But you don't seem to realize your own contribution to my displeasure. You're often careless, and almost always leave some portion of your duties undone."

Brys didn't think so, but there would be no benefit in arguing. He listened.

"You're getting old enough that you should be able to fulfill your responsibilities unsupervised. I will not speak more of this now."

Brys glanced down at the table, then looked back at Patter.

So, maybe it is that I'm twelve?

It still didn't seem like Patter – not the companionable, easy, and affectionate man he was used to.

"It's your transgression of last night that I want to address. Sneaking disobedience is utterly unacceptable, Brys. Do you understand?"

Brys nodded.

"Yes, Patter."

His voice sounded high and childish in his ears.

"Good. If I can't trust you, can't rely on you when you are not under my eye, then our life together as patter and son cannot work. I'll have to ask your Uncle Karl if he can take you. Or send you back east to your motter's sister – your Aunt Matilde."

Shock deprived Brys of utterance for a moment.

Then he stuttered, "B-but . . . w-we've always been together. I th-thought we always would be. P-partners."

Patter looked at him expressionlessly.

"I thought so too. But without trust, we cannot be."

His lips tightened. "Brys, I am not willing to embark on a course in which you disobey and I punish, and you disobey and I punish again."

The weight of Patter's gaze felt unbearable. Brys' eyes fell once more, stayed fixed on the table.

Patter's voice sharpened. "Do you understand, Brys? Your next disobedience, your next dishonesty, means you go."

His eyes flicked upward, seeking some sign of caring in Patter's face. There was none, only graveness and judgement.

"I understand," he responded huskily.

Patter said nothing, waiting for something more.

"I'm sorry, Patter," Brys mustered. And he was sorry, just not as sorry as Patter wanted him to be. "There won't be a next."

"Good. Good." Now Patter's face was lightening. "I believe you."

Miracles: was that actually a smile tugging at Patter's mouth?

"But, Brys, you know there must be a consequence." Warmth had returned to Patter's voice.

"Yes, I know," Brys agreed reluctantly.

"Very well. Are you ready to hear it?"

Finally, Patter was returning to the usual script they followed when Brys did something wrong.

"What is it, Patter?"

"You'll spend today and the next three sevendays hunting deadfall in the forest. You may have Jol's company, if you can persuade him to the task, but you'll take the hand cart immediately you've finished morning chores and return only when it's time for evening ones. Understood?"

Brys nodded.

Yes, he understood. And . . . it wasn't *so* bad, if only it hadn't been *four* sevendays. A whole month without leapfrog or hide-and-bide or ring toss or any of the other games he and Jol and Lars and the others enjoyed on the rest day.

He repressed a sigh.

At least Patter was normal again. The tension had left his voice, his face, and his movement.

He met Brys' gaze normally when he offered: "I'll pack your dinner pail while you step over to your aunt's, if you wish to talk with Jol."

Luckily, Jol was willing to join him in deadfall scrounging. The day would not be nearly so lonely and boring.

Brys scampered to pull the hand cart out from under the stairs and add a drop of oil to the left axle. The left wheel had started to squeal the last time the cart was used, and he didn't want to listen to it all day.

Jol was ready by the time Brys returned the oil can to its shelf.

They headed north into the forest. Glinhult had been built within a grove of Wych elms, but the boys soon passed into the endless stretches of pines that supplied the timber claim granted by the Queen to Patter and Uncle Karl.

The going was easy, since the land was flat around Glinhult's hill. Small thickets of rowan and juniper dotted the forest floor where enough sunlight trickled through, but deep shade cloaked most of the space under the evergreen canopy. The ferns and reindeer moss that thrived in it created little barrier to the hand cart's passage.

Brys found a small sapling gnawed down by beaver before they'd gone far, but he knew that the nearer reaches would be largely bare. Too many other Glinhulters scavenged near the hamlet for wood.

He broke the branches off the trunk, then knelt to saw pieces from one end, while Jol sawed at the other.

"You alright?" questioned his cousin.

"Yeah." *Why wouldn't he be?*

"You said you'd never seen Uncle Arn so . . . grim and flat . . . and . . ." Jol trailed off, then made another effort. "Scrounging deadfall seems pretty mild. I thought . . ." This time he didn't continue.

"Patter didn't take a stick to me, if that's what you mean."

By Jol's flush as he tossed pieces of sapling into the cart, that *was* what he'd meant. Brys added his wood to the cart, grabbed the pulling handle, and moved off. Jol fell in beside him.

"So, you scrounge deadfall for a day and that's it? My patter would do more than that, if I pulled what you did last night." Jol sounded envious.

"No," corrected Brys. "Every sevenday for the next month."

"Oh." Jol looked mollified. "Yeah. That's more like it."

Now Brys was indignant. "It would be, if that was all, but it's not."

Jol just looked at him, saying nothing.

"If I do anything like it again, Patter'll send me away, back east, to Aunt Matilde," Brys blurted.

"He wouldn't!" Jol looked disbelieving.

"I believed him. When he said it." Brys shivered at the memory. "You would too, if you'd seen him. Heard him. He was . . ." Brys didn't want to admit aloud just how scary Patter had been.

"Huh." Jol walked in silence for a while. "So, you gonna test him?"

"Patter won't give me another chance."

"Huh."

Jol said nothing more, and neither did Brys. He didn't really want to think about it. Patter was . . . kind again . . . ordinary, and Brys would take good care not to provoke him another time. He never wanted to see that unyielding expression on Patter's face, that was sure.

Jol interrupted his unspoken decisions with a smart rap on the forearm and a dash ahead. "Race you to the Alten Pool," he called.

"Hey! I've got the cart! How could I possibly beat you?"

Jol snickered and kept going, tossing over his shoulder, "Giving up without trying, mill rat?"

Brys rose to the bait. "I'm no more a mill rat than you, wood beetle!" But he gripped the hand cart more firmly and began to run while dragging it through the soft clutch of the ferns and lichens.

Jol got there first, of course, but Brys achieved his own victory when he succeeded in pining his cousin in an arm lock during the impromptu wrestling match that followed.

"I give! I give!" yelled Jol. "Don't break it!"

"Hah!" gasped Brys, and let him up. It was rare that he could beat his cousin. Jol's taller inches and broader shoulders gave him a decided advantage.

There were a lot of beaver-felled trees all around the Alten Pool and upstream along the rivulet that fed it, more than enough to fill the cart several times over. In undiscussed agreement, they completed the wood-gathering before lunch, then lingered by the water after eating. No point in bringing *two* cart loads, when one would satisfy Patter. And snatching half a sevenday with Jol would be almost better than a full one with Lars and the gang.

They tried leapfrog, but that wasn't so good with just two. And hide-and-bide got boring for the same reason. But swimming and ducking one another was fun, as was racing to see who could shimmy fastest to the top of a pair of twin Bythean pines.

It was during a second round of hide-and-bide (more satisfactory now, when they wanted something quieter) that he found it.

Jol was the seeker, and Bryce the bider. He'd gone downstream to the Alten Pool and past it, then upstream along a minute tributary to a smaller smidgeon of still water. It looked like some other Glinhult foragers must have been through, although why they'd left a scattering of sawn logs behind puzzled him.

But one of them had lost something even more precious.

It gleamed deep, deep blue in the reindeer moss – the color of the highest arch of the sky just after the evening star shone out at dusk. Small sparkles of gold against the smooth leather drew Brys' attention.

He picked it up.

It was a belt, finely crafted with double buckles, also of gold, and a gold keeper. The metallic scintillas in the leather were actually gold stars attached with rivets. The back of the belt was wide, nearly a full hand's span, while the front narrowed to two fingers' width.

Without thinking, Brys pulled his tunic up and strapped the belt around his waist over his shirt.

Ow! Each one of the riveted stars felt like a small pin-prick in the skin of his waist.

But the rest of him felt . . . different, strange.

He pulled his tunic down and jumped to reach the lowest branch of a large, old birch with multiple trunks.

He seemed to spring higher more easily than ever, and his hands caught their grip more securely. He hauled himself onto the branch as lightly as he might have pulled a mischievous kitten out of a basket of yarn. His arms and legs felt refreshed, full of energy. His torso felt ready for a hundred sit-ups. He climbed to the topmost branch that could bear his weight with scarcely more effort than he might have climbed the stairs at home.

It's a belt of strength, he marveled. *I've found a magic belt, just like in the legends of old!*

Jol eventually wandered into view below.

He checked under the trunk of a fallen pine, behind a tumble of boulders, within a rowan thicket, and beyond the cascade feeding the diminutive spring. Finally, being no stranger to hide-and-bide in the woods, he looked up.

"Hah! You hide, I ride, and now you're spied!"

Brys laughed and came out of the tree in a controlled tumble.

While Jol's eyes widened at this sample of daring, Brys charged him in an exuberant tackle. His cousin's automatic hook behind the ankle and twist while falling brought Jol down uppermost. In the past, the move resulted in Brys' defeat.

Not this time.

Brys dug his heels in beneath himself, gave a mighty heave, and flipped Jol into the pine needle duff.

Jol's surprised eyes widened still more. "What'd you do?" he gasped, and then tapped out as Brys completed a head lock.

"I'm stronger! I'm stronger! I'm stronger!" crowed Brys, letting his cousin up.

"You are not!" yelled Jol, stung and missing his meaning. "I've pinned you any day since solstice last, and you know it, you mingy mill rat!"

(They were all mill rats, really. Most of Glinhult's felled logs had to be milled into planks before the wagons hauled them east. That's why the hamlet existed.)

But Jol was used to winning, and losing twice in one day did not sit well. Yet Brys didn't mean he was stronger than *Jol*. Although . . . he was *now*, wasn't he?

"Lift this log!" he challenged.

It was a massive thing, suited to be the heart of a winter solstice fire, likely weighing eight stone or more.

"You can't lift that." Jol looked shocked and a touch confused.

"Can too! Can too!" Brys bubbled with the assurance that he *could* lift "that."

"My patter couldn't even lift it," insisted Jol.

Brys bent, gripped a protruding root at its

base, wriggled his other hand into a crevice at the other end, tightened his belly, and shoved upward with his legs. Like a dog pulled from a bog, the log came glueily upward. Brys stood balanced for a moment, then, in a further boast of his prowess, tossed his burden some five paces away. He glanced, pantingly triumphant, at his cousin.

Jol's face had whitened, and he was backing away.

"Well?" demanded Brys.

Jol shook his head. "You're bewitched. Or accursed. Or something worse. I don't know, but you're not –" he broke off, then concluded, swallowing some other word, "yourself."

Brys' ebullience ebbed. *Was* the belt accursed? Was *he* accursed, wearing it? In the excitement of discovery, he'd not considered . . . anything. But . . . *accursed*?

"Am not! Am too!" he countered Jol. "You just can't stand losing *twice.*"

Jol licked his upper lip. "Brys, wait."

"Hah! I won! I won!" Brys crowed again. "You're weak! You're weak!"

"You did not either win, you skunk!" Jol's qualms, whatever they were, evaporated under

Brys' continued trumpeting. "You cheated! Just like you cheated last night!" Jol's face was red now, not white.

"I did not either cheat! I won that second place fair and square!"

"But you wouldn't have won anything, if you hadn't cheated my Uncle Arn! You tricked your way into that rope climbing contest. So there! And I don't blame Uncle for threatening to send you away east. Who'd want to be step-motter to *you*? Liar!"

What? What was Jol talking about?

Well, lying, for one thing. Now Brys could feel his own face reddening in rage.

"I've never lied in my life! You mucky midden rat!" (A much nastier insult than the common "mill rat.") "Not even when Aunt Mersela asked me about Lars' broken toe. She thought it was *your* fault, but I confessed it was mine. You – you – troll-witch!"

His cousin narrowed his eyes, and Brys felt his stomach lurch at his own words. He was angry, yes, but . . . troll-witch was worse than an insult. It implied a serious crime. He shouldn't have said it, no matter what.

Jol's voice leveled in exactly the horrid way

that Patter's had last night. "I'm no troll-witch, but you just might be. Listen to yourself." Scorn crossed his face. "Enemies don't accuse each other like that, let alone friends and cousins. No wonder Uncle Arn is worried. Why would Briet Sigrunsdotter want *you* as a step-son?"

Jol turned his back abruptly and stalked off.

Brys felt his jaw drop.

He'd had fights with his cousin before. Of course. But mostly they were teasing taken too far. Or, if it were serious, they worked it out. Or let it go, turning real anger to mock fisticuffs. This – Jol simply walking off after serious censure – had never happened.

I think I really went too far.

Or was it the belt? Wanting to look at it again, he pulled his tunic off over his head, tossing the garment to the ground.

He stroked the belt's smooth leather. It was as deeply blue as he remembered. The buckles, keeper, and riveted stars as richly golden. But was the uncomfortable prickle of pins and needles around his waist stronger? Maybe.

A raspy, old man's voice interrupted Brys' investigations. "So, young un, was that dark-headed fella an old enemy or an old friend?"

Brys started and turned toward the speaker.

He was short, nearly a hand span shorter than Brys, but he wasn't a boy. His hair was a grizzled gray and grew in a wild mane around his face. His beard was equally wild, but thin. His voice had sounded genial, almost friendly, but his watery, pale blue eyes held a mad glitter. And his nose was long, his ears overlarge.

Was he, could he be, a troll?

Brys had never seen one . . . but this grandpatter – if he were one – bore the signs Brys had learned at school.

"A friend," he muttered in answer to the old man's question.

"I'd say he won't be a friend much longer, lessen you do some good groveling."

How much had this geezer heard? The whole stupid interchange?

"I know," Brys replied glumly. "We've been friends since we were babies. His motter – my aunt – was my wet nurse."

"Might be worth some grovelling then," concluded the stranger.

Was he a troll?

He seemed pretty normal, aside from his odd appearance, not crazy like trolls were said to be.

"I doubt grovelling'll be enough." Brys sighed. "I'm an idiot! Just an idiot! Gah!"

"Come take a cuppa tea with me, young un. I've seen a heap o' troubles worsen yourn, and I might have a few suggestions."

Brys eyed him suspiciously. *Was* he a troll?

"Or not." The old man seated himself on the log Brys had tossed. "M' name's Ryndal. Ryndal Vensson, but plain Ryndal's good enough."

"I'm Brys, Brys Arnsson." The courtesy came unthinkingly, but absently. His real worry carried more vehemence. "Do you really know how I can make things right with Jol?"

"Yer cousin, eh?" Ryndal tilted his head to one side and scrutinized Brys with his twinkling eyes. Maybe they weren't mad, just merry? "Well . . . lettin' some time go by afore you try is usually good. Let the other fella cool off, maybe even miss ye a bit. I bet yer already missin' Jol some."

"Yeah."

Brys shifted uncomfortably. He was missing Jol. But that wasn't why he was wriggling. The prickles around his waist *were* growing stronger. He wished he could just take the belt off, but it seemed rude to simply undress in front of Ryndal.

"Do you think Jol's missing me?" he asked.

"Maybe. Maybe not. Who was in the wrong, just now?"

Brys felt his face flush in embarrassment. "Me. I was boasting. And I just kept on, even after Jol made it plain he was sick of it." Brys shook his head. "It's just . . . even when we were younger and closer in size, I only beat him sometimes. And almost never since he turned thirteen. I was so excited this time." His voice sounded forlorn in his ears. "And it wasn't even true."

"What wasn't?" Ryndal looked puzzled.

"Beating him. It wasn't me. It was . . ." Brys didn't know why he hesitated, suddenly uneasy. "It was just luck," he finished.

"Hmm." Ryndal stood, sprightly despite his apparent age. "Well, Brys Arnsson, I'm headed home. I want that cuppa, even if you don't. But yer welcome to join me. Or not, as ye choose."

Brys surveyed his new acquaintance.

His suspicion was beginning to feel silly. *Ryndal's shorter and skinnier than me. Why am I afraid of him?*

"Is it far?" he asked.

"Just a quarter hour's walk."

Not far then.

"I'll come, Ryndal. Thanks."

The way lay farther upstream along the tributary that joined the outflow from the Alten Pool. Ryndal followed its winding course along the flat forest floor, nipping agilely over small boulders, detouring occasionally to go around rowan and juniper thickets.

Brys trailed him, not really marking the route, increasingly preoccupied by the needles circling his waist.

Ow! Ow! Ow!

Finally it dawned on him: now was the time to take the *shunning* belt off. *Ryndal's got his back to me. He'll never notice.*

Sias! The relief of it, once the leather dangled from his hand, was exquisite. But the pain had been more than mere discomfort. His shirt was dotted with blood where each star rivet had touched. *Huh!*

He wrapped the belt into a compact coil, but it was still too bulky to fit in the pocket of his trews, so he held it in one hand.

A few moments later, they rounded a stand of rowan, and Brys saw Ryndal's abode. It was nothing like the tree houses and stilt homes of Glinhult. A massive hunk of granite – seemingly plunked down in the forest by a cloud giant – rose steeply amidst a grove of aspens. A neat, shingled wall with a door and a window in it filled what must once have been a simple opening to a natural cave at the base of the stone hill. A stove pipe protruded from the hillcot's front wall, and a bird feeder topped a pole in the clearing.

Ryndal skipped to his front door, beckoning. "Welcome to Stenstuga, Brys. Do come in."

Inside, although the floor had been leveled and flagged, the rough cavern walls and ceiling remained in their natural state. But it was furnished like a normal home.

A tile stove squatted between the door and window. A round table and two chairs occupied the center of the space, while a freestanding cupboard – pushed against a side wall – held Ryndal's bed nook.

The back wall featured a massive riverstone hearth with a bread oven over the low fireplace. Niches corralled kindling and logs, and in-built shelves stocked jars of tea, honey, flour, and other staples.

A door quilt hung to one side of the hearth. Maybe covering a passage to a cellar?

Ryndal spooned loose tea into a teapot, then poured hot water into it from the kettle bubbling on the hearth. He gestured Brys to one of the chairs. "Honey?"

Brys sat and nodded. "Yes, please. Just one spoonful, though." He'd learned that most grownups assumed kids had a sweet tooth. And he did, but not for tea.

Ryndal replaced the kettle on its hook and took a pair of mugs down from his shelves. Grotesque imp faces peered out from around their handles. Brys couldn't decide if they were funny or scary. A bit of both, perhaps.

Where should he put his belt?

It'll just fall to the floor, if I set it on my lap.

He shrugged and set it on the table. It certainly wasn't going back on *him* anytime soon. He could feel the small wounds around his waist scabbing over, but the entire band of skin was tender.

Ryndal poured from the teapot into the mugs and pushed Brys' toward him along with a spoon to stir the honey well in.

"So, yer the younger cousin, are ye?" began his host.

"Yeah." Brys sipped his tea. It was scalding hot, but tasted just the same as Aunt Mersela's mint blend from her garden.

Was Ryndal watching him extra closely?

No, he decided. The old man was just awaiting more of an answer. "But it doesn't usually matter. Really, it never mattered." He gripped the table edge in sudden inspiration. "We always used to joke, Jol and me, that we were like Nils and Jan, the brothers in the Langladan Saga."

Ryndal frowned and shook his head slightly, so Brys explained.

"You know, when Jan attempted the glass hill to challenge the griffon at the top, Nils was his stirrup man. And after Nils dueled the wild unicorn in the faerie wood, Jan dunked him in the magic spring when he lay dying. They watched each other's back."

"You and Jol were always on the same side." Ryndal nodded.

Brys sighed. "I think we still are, except . . ."

"Except what?"

"Except this." Brys pointed to the coiled belt resting beside his tea mug.

"Mm?" Ryndal tilted his head, birdlike.

Did the glitter of his eyes grow more pronounced? *Was* that glint merriment? Or . . . something else?

"I found it in the forest," Brys confessed, prodding the leather with a finger.

"So, it's not truly yourn." A tiny smile curved Ryndal's lips.

"No," Brys agreed. "But that's not really the problem. It's . . ." He hesitated, then rushed on: "It's that I really *was* cheating. It's a belt of strength, and I couldn't have beat Jol right then without it. He had me fair and square. It was the belt that let me flip him and pin him."

He looked imploringly at Ryndal. Somehow, if this stranger understood and forgave him, then maybe Jol would too.

"Would you like me to examine it?"

Huh? That wasn't what Brys had been angling for. Aside from making Brys' cheating possible, the nature of the belt wasn't at issue. He stared at Ryndal, puzzled.

The old man perched at the front of his chair, eager, and the gleam in his eye *was* stronger.

Brys shrank back in his own chair, feeling the slight alarm provoked by this new friend – *was he a friend?* – edging toward . . . fear?

"What does the belt have to do with Jol forgiving me?" he asked warily.

"I think it might have something to do with it." Ryndal's bushy eyebrows were raised.

Oh.

Oh! Of course. Maybe it wasn't just a belt of strength. Maybe it was also a belt of lying or a belt of . . . of . . . corruption. Or something like that.

Brys straightened and leaned forward.

"Really? Could you check it? Find out if the *belt* made me act like such a . . . such a donkey?"

"Do you want me to?" Ryndal's eyes grew grave, but still held an unsettling gleam in their depths.

"Yes!"

"Very well. Hand it to me, please."

Brys complied.

Ryndal slowly uncoiled the blue leather and let it hang from one hand. He looked intently at Brys, a strange quirk to his mouth – mocking?

Then he pulled the belt behind his back, held it straight, seeming almost reluctant to clasp it round himself, took a deep breath, and quickly buckled it closed. A suppressed hiss of pain escaped him.

"I'm sorry! I should have warned you. It hurts, doesn't it?"

Ryndal, still with the odd look on his face, nodded slowly. "Yes. It stings."

Then he squared his shoulders, hopped briskly to the door and lowered the bar. Turning, he paused to contemplate Brys.

"What is it?"

The brightness in Ryndal's eyes rekindled and spread across the rest of his features.

"I'm hungry, young un." His tone was mild, but his hands reached out clawlike.

Brys' stomach felt sickly hollow.

Surely Ryndal couldn't mean . . . what he seemed to mean.

Brys' body assessed the situation much faster than his stunned thoughts. While his mind yet debated Ryndal's words in astonishment, his arms shoved him away from the table violently – knocking his chair over with a clatter – and his legs leapt toward the door quilt.

Please, please, please be a back door, a secret passage, a way out, any way out.

His frantic hands swept the fabric aside.

Not a door.

The quilt had hidden a *cage*, about the heighth and width of a door, equally deep, and fashioned from stout sapling trunks.

Brys spun to dash for the barred door, but Ryndal was on him: hairy, bony, and impossibly heavy.

Brys crashed to the floor.

Ryndal's breath stank. And the thrashing of his old man body as he blocked each of Brys' panicked bids for freedom was nauseatingly loathsome.

Brys made a final effort to squirm out from under his captor and then submitted as he felt Ryndal seize his head and twist. He went limp.

"That's better," purred Ryndal. "A shame to snap a brave lad's neck untimely."

Brys suppressed the shudder that tried to run through him.

Oh, Sias! He *is* a troll. *I should've known, should've guessed, should've run. When I first saw him.*

The weight pinning his shoulders down released him suddenly. Then a quick jerk dragged him up headfirst by the hair and flung him inside the cage.

Gasping from the force with which his ribs hit the flagstones, he saw Ryndal stretch to reach something out of sight while holding the barred door closed.

The item proved to be a heavy padlock.

The troll placed it around the first bar of the door and the adjacent bar of the cage, then guided the hasp home with a metallic click.

Brys was dazed. It had all happened so fast. His scalp burned from the yank to his hair, and his ribs felt bruised. *I should say something. Ask something. Persuade . . . somehow.* But no utterance came to him.

Ryndal was standing outside the cage staring in. Also without words, panting a little, and even yet with that odd brightness in his face. He nodded, turned on his heel, unbarred the hillcot door, and went out.

Released from Ryndal's stare, Brys found himself able to move. He pushed upright and scooted to lean against the hearthside bars of the cage.

Oh, Sias, what a mess I'm in!

How was it that he'd not known Ryndal was a troll? Every child in Silmaren learned the signs: elongated nose, enlarged ears, sagging skin, watery eyes, bent body. Ryndal had all those marks upon him. Somehow the reality was different from the picture Brys had formed in his mind.

And Ryndal was so short. And brisk. And friendly.

I didn't see it. Didn't see it at all. Not til he said . . . *that.* Now the repressed shudder shook him.

I'm hungry, young un.

What was Ryndal hungry for? A pet? A servant? Maybe just a whipping post?

Brys didn't want to admit he knew. The gross memory of the troll's stinking breath and heavy weight burgeoned and cloyed.

Brys scrubbed his hands across his face. Whatever Ryndal wanted, Brys *had* to escape.

He levered himself to his feet. Yes, he could stand – no bones broken – but his knees wobbled.

He checked the padlock. Its hasp was firmly seated in the locking mechanism. At the other side of the door, iron chains, welded closed into loops, served as hinges.

He grasped the bars and shook.

Everything rattled; no fine joinery here. But it was sturdy. And the door was tight enough that he couldn't squeeze through a gap between it and its frame.

He sank back to the floor, wrapping his arms around his shins, leaning his forehead on his knees. He shivered, even though this spot next to the hearth was overly warm. His thoughts circled wildly: have to escape, no escape, must escape, no escape.

A sound outside in the clearing brought his head up.

What was that? Was Ryndal returning? He shot to his feet and craned his neck, trying for a view through the window.

He could see the bird feeder – a trio of chaffinches clustered on its perches – and beyond it to the gap in the woods through which he and Ryndal approached the troll's hillcot. The portions of the clearing at the far sides were hidden from him, but . . . the chaffinches would have flown to safety, if a visitor – or his troll "host" – were present. Come to think, that abrupt crack, followed by a swishing rush and soft thump, tended to accompany the fall of a weak limb from a tree.

This exercise of logic restored him to sense.

So, he couldn't escape, but it was possible he didn't need to. Patter would come looking for him when Brys didn't arrive home for evening chores. Which – he gauged the shadows creeping across the clearing – would be soon.

The light would last a long while yet, but milking Pilka and Pehmea, washing the cheeses, and eating supper didn't wait on nightfall. Especially in high summer.

He envisioned Patter rounding up Uncle Karl and Lars' patter and some others.

They'd bring lanterns just in case the search went on after dark. And they'd know where to look. Jol could tell them where he and Brys had been gathering deadfall. Surely they'd fan out from the Alten Pool. And Ryndal's home wasn't far.

They'd find him. Of course, they'd find him.

He drew a breath of relief. They might even arrive before Ryndal got back from wherever he'd gone.

Brys uncurled his body, crossed his legs tailor fashion, and stretched his arms overhead. He'd grown cramped without realizing it. He was also . . . hungry.

The word chilled him.

I'm hungry, young un.

Ryndal's matter-of-fact tone had carried an awfulness in its very moderation.

Brys shook himself as though he were a retriever drying off after a dip in a lake. He wouldn't think about it. Patter or Uncle Karl would be here soon, and then all would be well.

Or would it?

Suppose Patter *didn't* organize a search party? What if he decided Brys were playing truant?

Oh, Sias, no!

But it seemed all too possible. Patter would think Brys was disobeying once more. Repeating the disobedience of last night to shave today's punishment. Oh, Sias, yes!

A footfall outside arrested his descent into frozen panic.

This time it was Ryndal. He carried an armful of sticks in through the door, nodded companionably to Brys, deposited his load in one of the hearth nooks, and went back out for a second and then a third load.

After dusting his clothes of bark pieces and sawdust, the troll started supper preparations, adding some charcoal to the fire, grinding hazel nuts with a mortar and pestle. He added water and the paste to a pot, then stirred the nut porridge over the heat of the hearth.

Watching these homely tasks, some of Brys' tension waned. When Ryndal pushed a bowl of porridge under the cage door – it barely slid through – he plucked up enough courage to ask, "Couldn't you just let me go home?"

Ryndal looked startled, almost as though the porridge pot had grown mouth and tongue to speak. He scratched his head. "Why would I do that, young un?"

"Because I want it. Because I've never done you any harm. Because it would be right." *Maybe I can talk my way out of this.*

Ryndal shook his head.

Maybe not.

"But ye have harmed me."

What?

"Ye stole me belt." Ryndal was still wearing it, although smudges of the blood it drew stained his tunic at the lower edge of the leather.

The troll seated himself at the table and began to eat.

"It's yours?"

"Yep. I usually take it off between bouts o' wood choppin'. It does sting, ye know."

Yes, he knew. But! "Why didn't you say? I would have given it back!"

Ryndal looked at him shrewdly. "Would ye now?"

Brys blushed.

Would he?

He *thought* so, but he wouldn't have wanted to. And maybe . . . unfortunately . . . he would have claimed finders-keepers. Or worse, pretended to disbelieve Ryndal.

"Uh huh." The troll's voice was knowing.

"Hard to give up power once ye've held it in yer hand."

"But I didn't know. And I *didn't* steal it. You have it back now. With my own hand, I put it into yours. Oh, please, let me go! Why wouldn't it be right?"

"Because I'm not wishin' to starve, young un. Nut porridge isn't enough to keep a man. It takes a bit o' meat, now and again."

Brys stared at the troll. He sat there quite calmly, spooning supper into his mouth. *Divine Mother.* Neither pet nor servant nor scapegoat. Ryndal wanted *dinner*.

Brys felt sick. He put his own spoon back into his full bowl, unable to contemplate swallowing.

"You can't mean that," he asserted, knowing Ryndal *did* mean that.

"Why not? Me bread oven's big enough. I just need to chop a bit more wood. Make sure I've got enough to get it good and hot. And keep it good and hot while ye roast."

Sias within! Brys inched himself backwards, fetching up against the rear bars of the cage.

"Eat up, young un. I'll want to wash that bowl afore I turn in. But ye've a while to do it, if yer not hungry yet."

Ryndal hopped to his feet, collected the porridge pot from the floor where he'd placed it to cool, and took it outside with his own empty bowl. Evidently he did his washing in the stream.

I'm hungry, young un.

Brys tried to drag his thoughts away from Ryndal's words as they echoed in his memory. *I have to stop thinking about that. I need to think about what I can do.*

But what could he do?

He was in the presence of a troll. Even could he escape his cage, how could he defeat Ryndal's terrible strength, augmented as it was by the enchanted belt? And even if Ryndal eventually took that off – it *was* painful to wear – how could Brys withstand the potent troll-magic that Ryndal surely commanded?

How did *I miss his troll-hood?*

The answer – an unwelcome one – popped abruptly into his thoughts.

I didn't miss it. Not really.

He'd known something was wrong. Felt that Ryndal was not to be trusted. He'd almost not answered Ryndal's first question. Almost declined his invitation to tea. Almost stayed silent about the belt. Almost . . . listened to that inner whisper of peril, of prudence. Almost, but not quite.

I wanted a magic solution, he admitted.

An easy way to repair things with Jol. A shortcut to physical strength. A sure way to make Patter . . . always be Patter.

And he'd sensed that Ryndal had the power to give him all these wishes. Likely a troll *could*. But never *would*.

Brys gritted his teeth.

He'd been a fool. Maybe a few things in life came free, dropped like magic into a day. But the best things – a friend's trust, useful skills, a patter's love – didn't work that way. You got more than you'd actually earned, yes, but you still had to do your part.

With Jol, he needed to apologize. And really mean it. And trust that Jol's friendship was strong enough that the shower of obnoxiousness from Brys hadn't withered it. Which it was. Not that he meant to abuse that loyalty, but he trusted Jol all the way down to the ground.

Jol would never betray him.

As for physical prowess . . . well, that would come with time and growing. Patter was physically strong. Likely Brys would be too.

And he was getting cleverer at wrestling. Jol was bigger, but wrestling wasn't all muscle might. Brys had won a few matches in the past, and he'd likely win more in the future.

If he had a future.

He glanced at the window. Had Ryndal gone off to chop more wood? Left the dishes to dry in the slight breeze?

Brys looked at his own nut porridge again.

I should eat. I'll think better, if my stomach's not empty.

True, but he still felt sick.

Just try one bite, he urged himself.

It was good. Ryndal had cooked a savory version, adding salt and umami herbs. Brys' nausea vanished as his very real hunger bloomed.

He scraped the bowl clean just as Ryndal arrived with, indeed, more logs. *Those remnants I thought other Glinhulters left must have been his — Ryndal's.* Huh.

The troll saw Brys' empty bowl. "Good job, young un." He scooped it out of the cage and took it outside, returning shortly with the other dishes as well, all clean. "Do ye want a pillow? I've got an extra."

"I guess."

Did he want one? It hardly seemed to matter. He didn't plan on sleeping.

He'd try chewing his way out, if he had to!

Wait a moment. Chewing? He wouldn't need to chew.

Ryndal hadn't checked Brys' pockets. Which meant . . . his pocket knife should still be there! He almost moved his hand to check.

Not now, you fool! He's looking at you!

"Oh, I'll not be roasting ye til the morrow." Ryndal reassured him.

Sias!

The troll continued: "I'll start building me fire afore the dawn, o' course, but ye may as well rest comfortable tonight."

Brys didn't want to hear these plans, but he supposed it was good to know that he *did* have time in which to effect his escape. He accepted the pillow that Ryndal pulled from the drawer below his bed nook and stuffed through the cage bars.

"The hearth'll keep ye warm, but if ye did want a blanket, I can spare one."

Brys nodded. He didn't need a blanket either, but perhaps he might use it to muffle the sounds of the whittling he hoped to do once Ryndal slept.

He longed to slip his fingers into his trews pocket.

Was the knife there? He couldn't remember pocketing it this morning, but why would he not have? He carried it always. You never knew when a sharp blade might come in handy. Like now!

Ryndal maneuvered the blanket into the cage, then fetched a canister from a shelf along with a pipe, and began preparing a smoke. Once the pipe was filled, he went back into the open air. Brys could see the troll's back through the window. There was a bench under it, he remembered.

Ryndal blew a few smoke rings.

Brys shoved a hand in his pocket.

Yes!

Sias be praised! He could escape. Or try to.

No, I will. I'll get out of this cage. I'll get out of this hillcot. And I'll get home. I'll stab him, if I have to.

But not now.

Ryndal would simply take the knife away, if he saw it. Brys moved his hand away from his pocket. It was hard to do nothing. Waiting, just waiting, for a troll to roast you alive – no!

I'm not waiting for roasting. I'm waiting for Ryndal to sleep.

Which gave him an idea.

It might be futile, or just unnecessary, but why not give Ryndal the impression that Brys had given up? Likely the troll was too shrewd, but still. Brys spread the blanket on the floor of the cage, placed the pillow to one side – away from the hearth – and lay down.

The cage was too small to permit him to straighten, but the softness of the blanket atop the flagstones was a relief. He closed his eyes. It would fool no one, but he didn't want to see this place anyway.

I'll plan my escape.

How would he accomplish it?

Wait till Ryndal goes to bed, then wait a while longer. Whittle through one of the bars encircled by the padlock. Ease the padlock through the gap, and open the door. Tiptoe to the hillcot door and unbar it. Open it and slip out. Walk softly until he was far enough away that he couldn't be heard. Yes!

Would that really work? Could he be quiet enough? Would Ryndal wake up amidst it all?

He shook his head.

I'll just do my best.

He opened his eyes again. The light was beginning to go. The clearing outside was wholly in shadow. The sky above the treetops glowed golden.

Inside, the dim radiance from the dying fire flickered.

Ryndal still sat on his bench in the open air, staring at nothing, and taking the occasional puff of his pipe.

Brys sat up and stretched. Then stood and stretched some more.

It wasn't enough.

He wanted to climb a tree, wrestle a friend, or run races with Lars and the gang.

Sitting still, lying still, standing still was getting old.

But when he heard Ryndal at the door, he sat abruptly and dove for his pillow.

"Asleep, lad?" Ryndal's voice sounded kind, except for that note of . . . hunger . . . that underlay it.

"Mmm," answered Brys.

Dusk had arrived, and the fire was nearly out. The corner holding his cage was very dark. He doubted Ryndal could see that he didn't look sleepy at all.

"I'll wake ye when it's time. Sleep deep, Brys."

Sias! As though he'd be getting up for morning chores!

He cracked his eyes open.

Ryndal was rummaging in the drawer under his bed nook. Evidently the troll wanted extra covers for himself. Blanket in hand, he drew open one shutter, nipped up onto the mattress, and pulled the shutter closed. A snick of metal told Brys that that the troll had some sort of lock inside.

Good. A bit of delay, if Ryndal *did* wake up.

Another sound hushed from the bed nook: an internal curtain? Better and better.

Brys squinted, trying to see more clearly in the growing dark. Were the bed shutters solid? Not louvered? He hadn't noticed earlier, and now he couldn't tell, but he thought . . . *not!*

Sneaking away began to seem more practical.

His hand itched to pull out his pocket knife.

Wait, he counseled himself. You've got to give Ryndal a chance to go to sleep.

He turned onto his back with his feet flat and his knees poking up.

There was still a chance Patter would arrive with a search party. But he wasn't going to wait on rescue from others. He would rescue himself.

Because, even if the Glinhulters were out in force, would they find Ryndal's cot? And Brys inside it? They'd missed this place for all the time Ryndal had lived here. They might miss it now also.

He shivered. Not from any chill.

I won't be waiting for Patter, he reassured himself.

Reaching for bravado, he added: if he *is* searching for me, *I'll* find *him* in the forest on my way home.

Although . . . if? *If!* Of course Patter would be searching. Even if he did think Brys were playing truant.

How had he ever believed Patter might abandon him to a night in Gosstrand's vast forest?

A memory of the time when he was very small and had gotten stuck up in a tree swirled through his thoughts. It had been daytime, but Patter had somehow known something was wrong, even before Aunt Mersela – who was watching him – realized Brys was missing.

Patter turned the mill over to the foreman and left in a hurry.

And searched the entire hamlet, until he found Brys, paralyzed with fright in the branches of the tallest Wych elm on the hill.

Patter had climbed up to him so swiftly and gripped him so securely in the circle of one arm. They were back on firm ground moments later, and Patter spent the rest of the day home, comforting Brys.

And then insisted he climb another tree – a shorter one!

Brys felt himself grinning.

Suddenly he knew that Patter's threat to send him east to Aunt Matilde was just that: a threat. Despite his surface calm, Patter had still been mad enough to spit wood chips. And . . . Brys had to admit his sneaking out to the solstice was but the last of a series of transgressions.

His turn watching the Glinhult reindeer, he'd left the herd untended when he found he'd forgotten his dinner pail. And Patter had merely cautioned him reasonably when he encountered Brys running home at noontide.

Then he and Jol locked Lars in the garden storage. They were playing brigands and soldiers, and the garden storage made an excellent castle dungeon. But then Einar went by on his new stilts, and he and Jol ran after him and stayed watching his antics, forgetting all about Lars.

Patter heard thumping when he got home from the mill.

And let Lars out.

He'd been reasonable about that too. And again when Brys shirked house chores the entire week before the school promotion exams. It hadn't been the shirking, Patter explained, but the not communicating that was the problem.

I'm still behaving like a child, he realized. As though the rules are there to break or get around, and doing the minimum to get by is enough.

It wasn't that he slacked a lot. Or avoided chores often. Mostly, he did do . . . his fair share. Sometimes even more.

It was his attitude that needed work.

He needed to stop treating . . . not life, but other people . . . like players in a game where there were points to be won or lost. He'd been winning. Collecting points by doing his chores and his homework and helping the widow next door.

But he needed to do those things, because . . . because . . . it was good to help others. And to be helped in turn.

It was part of being human – *not* being a troll – to live in community, to give, to cooperate. No wonder Patter had been so angry. It wasn't just the disobedience.

A faint sound from the troll's bed nook reached him. Was that a snore?

It came again.

Yes! Ryndal was sleeping.

Brys felt for his knife, drew it out, and unfolded the blade.

His cage was largely dark, but the glow of coals from the hearth illumined the front bars. He touched the door edge, then its frame. The frame felt thinner. He shifted the padlock out of the way and started digging with his blade.

The wood was tougher than he'd suspected, and the whittling made noise. Not a lot, but it wasn't silent. It sounded like a mouse gnawing at wainscoting.

But Ryndal's faint snores continued unabating.

With his fingertips, Brys investigated the notch he was creating.

Still small, but this *was* working. And he need not be so precise as if he were carving an owl or a hawk or a chaffinch. Big, ragged chunks were just fine for his purpose.

He started in again, pausing occasionally to push the shavings under his blanket.

Scrape, scrape. Scrape, scrape.

Ryndal's snores stopped when Brys was halfway through the frame bar.

He dropped to the blanket-padded floor, hiding his knife under his pillow.

But the troll stayed behind his bed shutters and eventually slept again. Perhaps he'd never really awoken, just changed position. But the resumed snores were reassuring.

Brys made it the rest of the way through the bar, and the snores were still sounding. The padlock slid through the tight gap just as he'd imagined, a steady pressure and then a sudden "thunk" as it sprang loose.

He eased the barred door open and slipped out, keeping his open knife gripped in his right hand.

He crept toward the front door, setting his feet down toe first as he stepped.

Maybe he should have taken his boots off.

Sneaking would be easier in stocking feet. But he wanted to be able to run once he was outside. If he needed to.

He rounded the table and saw that Ryndal had not barred the front door.

Excellent.

A flicker of movement caught the corner of Brys' vision.

What?!

No, not the bed cupboard.

Something outside.

He moved to the window to look. And saw Jol looking in, wild eyed, with most of his curling hair escaped from the tie that usually corralled it in a bushy horsetail down his back.

Brys jerked his finger to his lips in a frantic gesture for silence, but Jol wasn't looking any more.

"Brys! Why didn't you come home? Sias within!"

Then his cousin was tumbling through that unbarred door at the same moment that Ryndal tumbled out of his bed cupboard.

Brys leapt for Jol, trying to push him outside, but succeeded only in knocking him over.

"Run, Jol!" he yelled, miraculously keeping his own feet, trying to pull Jol back to his. "It's a troll!"

A bony thumb and forefinger clamped onto his ear. Brys jerked his head, feeling the thumbnail gouging deeply as he shook it off.

He stumbled forward, dragging Jol with him.

He was outside!

But Jol remained snarled in a heap on the threshold.

Brys bent to get a better grip on his cousin's arm. And met Ryndal, stooping for the same purpose.

"Ah, ah, ah," chastised the troll, smirking. "I wouldn't."

Brys ignored him, levering Jol up.

And Ryndal let go! Yes!

But the troll didn't back away as Brys somehow expected.

Jol found his balance, and Brys grabbed his hand, taking his first running step.

Then he heard Ryndal's shout behind them: "Stop, halt, be still! Flee not, my will! Wait late in my hill! Heat meat for my fill!"

A flash of acrid, orange light confused his vision.

Then his legs stiffened, abruptly immobile.

This time, he fell, and Jol with him.

He swept his knife arm aside – thank Sias he could move that – frantically trying to avoid stabbing his cousin in their tangled topple.

Could he hide the knife before Ryndal saw it?

Pressing it closed against his thigh, he slid it into *Jol's* pocket and let go the haft.

Ryndal approached, more menacing than he'd been before.

Brys struggled to rise, *run*, but his legs wouldn't move.

Ryndal loomed above him. The troll looked pleased.

"Never known me larder to be so full. Excellent!" Then his face lowered. "But running away. Sneaking! Ah, ah, ah. That won't do." He sounded querulous, like a sleepy grandpatter scolding an errant grandson. "Up with ye now."

Brys found himself climbing to his feet and shuffling back into Ryndal's hillcot. It felt natural, as though Patter had caught him slipping out for a moonlit ramble, except for the corner of his mind shouting: *Turn and run, fool!* Jol came with him, Ryndal chivying behind.

The troll ran his gnarled hands over the broken bar of the cage, and the wood healed under his touch. Next he brushed his fingertips across all the unbroken bars.

Did they change color?

It was hard to tell in the dim glow from the quiescent coals in the hearth.

"In ye go, lads."

Following Jol, Brys filed obediently through the door frame into the cramped space.

Ryndal drew a key from the pocket of his nightshirt – evidently he'd changed within his bed nook, although the blue belt still encircled his waist – unlocked the padlock, repositioned it around the cage door and frame, and fastened the hasp once again.

Then he gestured sharply with one hand, and Brys felt his limbs become his own to command.

His legs nearly buckled, and he clutched the cage bars to avoid falling. Jol was less fortunate, slithering abruptly down to the blanket with a thump.

"That's better." Ryndal nodded. "But no more mischief, young uns. Ye'd best get a good night's sleep afore sunup. It's not far off."

Brys shivered and gritted his teeth.

If only he'd been just a bit faster. Made it outside before Jol arrived. Or even gotten to the window quick enough to signal before Jol called out.

He'd *almost* escaped.

But almost only counted in games. This was no game.

And now Jol was also headed toward the bread oven. Brys glared at Ryndal, who seemed oblivious to his hostility.

The troll glanced at the dark clearing through the window behind him.

"I suppose it's not so bad ye woke me. Time to be heatin' the oven about now. And I can get a nap afore it's time to add a second serving o' logs to the fire."

He bent to stir the coals, then began placing kindling atop them. As the light grew brighter from the hearth, Brys could see blood stains wetting Ryndal's nightshirt at the lower edge of the charmed belt. The wounds inflicted by its enchantment must continue to worsen the longer it was worn.

Would Ryndal take it off for some relief?

Even if he did, could Brys and Jol prevail against his normal strength? The troll looked spindly, but even were he as puny as he appeared, his magic was invincible.

Brys could feel Jol shivering against his legs, crouched there on the cage floor, but he didn't look down.

I'll deal with Jol after I've seen Ryndal retire to his nap.

He realized that he didn't feel daunted, even though he should. *I haven't given up.* And he wouldn't.

Once the fire was truly blazing, sparks snapping and flames leaping, Ryndal moved another armful of logs from their niche and stacked them on the floor, ready for immediate use. Then he paused, scrutinized the results of his labor, looked fixedly at Brys, and said, "That'll do."

He rummaged in the drawer under his bed nook and pulled out a clean nightshirt.

Brys looked down at Jol.

His cousin had stopped shivering, although it probably wasn't because of the heat rolling off the hearth, but he still huddled his arms around his legs and body.

He's shocked just like I was when Ryndal first captured me. Wishing he'd wake from this horrific nightmare.

Brys pressed his lips together. He still didn't know how he was going to defeat Ryndal. It seemed impossible. But he felt renewed determination to try. And a nudge, a hint, a wink – something – made him feel it was possible.

He looked up again. Ryndal was finally removing the belt of strength and hanging it on a nail to the left of the hearth. Was it within reach? Brys didn't think so, but didn't give it much thought.

Ryndal's nightshirt was sodden where the belt had lain, soaked with blood. Yet he'd given no sign of the pain it must have caused.

He still evinced no symptoms of incapacity.

Instead he hopped into his bed nook, drew the inner curtain, rustled about behind it, threw the dirty nightshirt onto the flagstones, thrust out an arm to pull the bed shutter closed, and – apparently – lay down.

Jol looked up, lips opening for comment.

Brys put a finger to his own lips and shook his head. *Wait.*

This time Jol saw and nodded.

Good.

Brys couldn't understand why their captor did so little to prevent his prisoners from attempting escape – well, overwhelming power might be why the troll wasn't worried, didn't want to bother – but it still seemed prudent not to announce their intention.

He tapped Jol's shoulder and made gestures showing his desire to sit. His cousin scooted over to make room, and Brys sank down, putting a finger to his lips again.

He almost fell asleep before Ryndal's snores indicated the troll was enjoying his intended nap.

Brys' eyes snapped open.

Jol was staring at him wide-eyed, no doubt incredulous that he could doze. He smiled. *I don't feel like a victim*, he realized. Although he had during his first sojourn in the cage.

Keeping his voice to a low murmur, he moved his head right up to Jol's ear and said, "I put my knife in your pocket. Can I have it?"

Jol's wide eyes went wider, but he produced the knife.

Brys tested it on a cage bar. Nope. Ryndal had done something to the wood, and it was tougher than before. His blade could score the bark, but not carve even the smallest chip from it. The cage was secure.

He stood and eeled an arm out out between two of the bars. If he could just reach that belt, it mightn't give him strength enough to breach the cage, but it could permit him to stun Ryndal once outside of it.

Nope.

His fingertips just missed brushing the blue leather.

But . . . what about his knife arm?

He wriggled his left hand back inside the bars, then tried to maneuver his right out through them. It couldn't be clenched, fist-like, around his knife, no. But pinning the knife between thumb and flattened palm got his hand through the gap, and then he could rearrange his grip with the help of his other hand.

He pressed his torso sideways against the cage, forcing his arm through narrowness to his shoulder.

Almost . . . almost . . . there!

His knife tip barely touched the leather.

He leaned a little harder, and the metal sank into the cobalt surface. He dragged his hand downward – still outstretched – and a ragged line of undyed suede followed the progress of his blade.

The cage bars were digging uncomfortably into his upper arm. His fingers felt numb and a little tingly. He tightened his grip and tried to continue his damage to the enchanted belt.

The knife slipped from his fingers and fell – click – on the floor.

He sagged against the cage, then straightened and retrieved his arm. Ryndal's snores buzzed without interruption.

"Will he notice?" Jol murmured. "The troll?"

Brys nodded. "Yeah. I'll try and reach it when my arm stops tingling. I think my knife fell a little closer, because of the angle I was cutting."

He massaged his shoulder, rotated it, then let it hang. Feeling was returning.

He motioned Jol to the rear of the cage while he knelt at its front and inserted his arm between the bars once again. After his hand and forearm were through, he maneuvered himself flatter to the floor, then walked his fingers toward the knife.

Closer, closer.

And, yes, it was just within reach.

Delicately he pushed the haft toward him, then folded it in his palm and drew it inside the cage.

"Do you want to try and stab him? When he gets us out? Or would you rather I did?" Brys asked his cousin.

"Uh." Jol looked nonplussed. "You seem like you know what you're doing. You keep it."

Brys folded it and put it back in his own pocket.

So: cage tested, belt damaged, and knife retrieved. What else should he be doing?

I'm ready. But Jol isn't.

That should be next then. But how? Just exhorting a friend to be brave wouldn't make him so.

He turned to face his cousin.

Jol was just as disheveled from his night time passage through the woods as he was when he appeared at Ryndal's window: hair wild with twigs, clothes torn, eyes strained. And – critically – lacking the confidence that usually backed his gaze. How to restore it?

"I owe you," Brys began, voice low.

Jol's brow wrinkled.

"I *was* a rat. Earlier."

Now Jol looked exasperated.

Better.

"Never mind that!" He aimed an elbow at Brys' ribs, but pulled it before contact. Likely worried about the noise a scuffle might produce. "I was a rat myself. What are we going to do about this?" He gestured at the cage, then the bed nook. "About him? I don't want to be some troll's breakfast."

That was supposed to be flippant, but the quaver at the end spoiled it. At least Jol was trying.

"Me neither."

"You got a plan? 'Cause I sure don't." His cousin sounded pugnacious now. Even better.

"I think this is one of those times when a plan doesn't help much. Patter says you just have to be ready for opportunity. But you have to be *ready*. Or the moment'll pass you by." He glanced sharply at Jol. "Are you ready, Jol Karlson? 'Cause I am. And I need you to be."

A slight smile curled Jol's mouth. "That's Uncle Arn's line, alright. I can just hear him." He drew a slow breath. "I suppose I was a useless goof when I got here."

"You weren't expecting a troll. Who would be?"

"No, but I didn't have to make a racket and wake him up. And then shrivel into a sniveling baby when he spelled me." Jol shook his head and pressed his lips together. "I think *I* owe *you*. You'd have gotten away, if I hadn't yelled."

"Maybe."

"Next time – well, I hope there isn't a next time! Not like this. But I aim to do more looking before I leap – or yell – if we get out of this, shun it!"

"Look, Jol, done is done. Just –"

"Don't do it again," interrupted Jol. "And I won't. But, Brys, I *will* be ready. If all I can do is be furious, then I'll be furious. But if his troll-magic leaves me any room for a punch or a kick or . . . or a chair smashed over his head, I'll fight."

"Then we're ready."

"As we can be." Jol wrinkled his nose. "Why'd you scratch that belt? What good will it do? Besides make him mad?"

"Might not do anything, but I figure any hurt to his stuff might give us . . . well, not an edge, but something."

"Huh."

"Was anyone besides you searching for me, Jol?"

"Oh, Sias! Only all of Glinhult!"

"Really?"

"Just about. Even my motter and Froiken Singrunsdotter insisted on joining the party. If there's anything to find in the forest, they'll find it." Jol shook his head. "Course they'll be just that extra mad when they do find us."

"I'll take any kind of mad, if they'd only walk through Ryndal's front door right about . . . now!"

"Me too. But they won't. Most went upstream, a few down. And the rest are combing the stretch between the stream and the hamlet."

"Then we'll find them."

"Yup."

They sat in silence for a bit, listening to the troll's snores.

Brys noticed a slight grayness at the window, a lightening to the dark sky. Dawn was approaching.

He yawned, wriggled all over to be sure he wasn't too stiff, and glanced at Jol.

"What did you say his name was?" Jol asked.

Before Brys could answer, Ryndal swept his nook curtain aside, pushed the pillow-end shutter open, and hopped out.

"Rise and shine, young uns. Morning's here."

Brys climbed to his feet, Jol following.

Ryndal paused in front of the cage. "I doubt I can fit ye both in the oven at once. Who wants to go first?" he queried, for all the world as though he were proposing a treat!

"I'll go first," Brys volunteered sturdily, remembering that he was the one with the pocket knife. What *had* happened to Jol's? Not that it mattered. He didn't have it.

"Alright then. That's settled." Ryndal carried on with refueling the fire. "We'll just let that heat the bricks a tad more, perhaps have tea" – he swung the kettle closer to the flames – "and get on with things."

Brys stiffened, anticipating Ryndal's move to open the cage. But the troll didn't. Instead, he disappeared back into his bed nook to dress, then gathered his blood-stained nightshirts and yesterday's clothes, and stuffed the garments into a basket hamper. "I don't suppose ye'll behave, if I just invite ye to the table, will ye?"

Brys said nothing, but Ryndal answered his own question. "O' course not."

He sighed and raised his left hand. "So." Then in a weary voice: "Sit still, do my will. Be not shrill, no thrill. Drink tea with me. Then look, and cook."

A brief flicker of orange light flared from the troll's palm, but Brys felt nothing.

He tensed again, could sense Jol shifting his weight forward onto the balls of his feet. And now Ryndal did unlock the cage and swing its door open.

Brys lunged.

Except he didn't.

Nothing resulted except a mild step toward the table, followed by another.

His heart hammered as he sought control of his limbs, but his feet simply marched him to a chair, where he sat. Jol did the same at the other chair, while Ryndal pulled up a three-legged stool for his own perch.

The troll fixed tea, pouring out three mugs.

Outside, the clearing grew fully visible in the gray light presaging the sun's leap above the horizon. Brys sipped, mouth and fingers calm, thoughts and feeling anything but.

Shun it!

The relaxation of his muscles told his mind that all was well. Which felt so very odd. His mind kept wanting to believe his body, but it shouldn't.

Death was a moment away – unless he got that opportunity Patter spoke of in his exhortations to be ready.

Brys sipped again, glancing at Jol. His cousin looked equally relaxed, but with a similar horror lurking in his eyes.

Ryndal drained half his mug, then set it down and stood.

"The oven should be about ready."

He moved to the hearth and opened the iron hatch above the fireplace.

Heat rolled out of it, making the already too-warm room more so.

"Yep." He closed the hatch, paused with his head tilted to one side, looking at Brys, then took the blue belt from its nail. "I reckon I'll need extra strength to boost ye up to it."

Brys tried another lunge – this time up from his chair – and again did not succeed.

Shun it! I'm about to be roasted alive without lifting a finger to stop it.

Had Jol attempted an abortive attack also? And failed? His face was pale enough.

Ryndal stood with his enchanted belt held straight behind his back as he had the day before. This time Brys knew why. The troll's waist must be a band of scabbed skin. It would more than sting when the star rivets made contact.

And it did.

Ryndal hissed and closed his eyes as the belt tongue slid home through its keeper. Then he staggered, as though his entire left side had gone numb.

He didn't have time to do more.

The unnatural relaxation that gripped Brys (and Jol) fled on the instant.

Brys shot to his feet, and his pent readiness did all that Patter had promised. It was as though he and his cousin had planned and practiced all through the dark hours before dawn.

Jol flew to the oven hatch and yanked it open, while Brys rocketed into the teetering troll, knocking him flat.

The next thing Brys knew, Jol was at his side, and they were boosting Ryndal up together, bundling him into the scorching maw of the oven, and slamming its hatch shut.

Brys leapt for the hillcot door, dragging Jol with him – except that Jol seemed to be leaping and dragging Brys – fully expecting Ryndal to burst out of the oven spouting death-defying troll-magic.

Front door.

Front steps.

Bird feeder and clearing – suddenly dappled golden as the sun rose and shone through the trees.

It all rushed by in a confused, panicky blur.

But no avenging troll-mage chased on their heels.

Brys kept running, even when the stitch in his side grew knife-like. He didn't notice Jol slowing either.

Finally, when they reached the Alten Pool, he tripped and went sprawling.

The ground came up hard, knocking the wind out of him.

He lay, cheek down, struggling for breath.

When he caught it, he burst into wracking sobs which lasted only three heartbeats, and then pushed himself upright.

Jol was returning from where his unreasoning legs had carried him. "You alright? Break anything?"

Brys wriggled his feet, shifted his shoulders. He felt bruised all over, but everything moved.

"Nah. Yeah. You?"

"Think so. Come on!" He grabbed Brys' arm and hauled him up. "We need to find somebody."

They walked, listening for sounds of pursuit. Or sounds of Glinhult searchers. But none came.

"Where is everybody?" complained Jol.

"Probably looking west when they didn't find me east. Or" – Brys felt a grin stretching his cracked lips – "they're just now entering Ryndal's hillcot. Hah!"

"Ryndal was his name?"

"Yeah."

But Brys wasn't thinking about the troll.

He would, he knew. Troll insanity was . . . a whole 'nother deal, not a thing like reading about it in a school book. And his memory of the feel of Ryndal's spindly body – so different from its hairy weight when augmented by the enchanted belt – as he and Jol lifted the troll up to his death sickened him in a way wholly different from Ryndal's brutal capture of himself.

But he would sort that out later. *At least I'm alive. And that's good!*

Right now he wanted to know something else.

"Does my patter really want to marry Briet?"

Jol laughed, surprised.

"Yeah, I think so. I heard him talking with Motter and Patter when they thought I was asleep. Do you mind?"

"Are you kidding? When we were all nursery babies being taught by her in our first schooling year, everybody kept thinking she was my motter. And she still gives me presents on my name-day and for winter solstice."

He wouldn't mention that he reciprocated. No need for Jol to know . . . well . . . everything.

"Huh."

"Huh, yourself!"

And Brys aimed a friendly punch at his cousin's ribs.

THE END

Months of the Year

Janary winter

Falnary late winter

Nerich early spring

Thyril spring

Ponce late spring

Joiesse early summer

Labra summer

Jube late summer

Sanember early autumn

Ionaber autumn

Noulember late autumn

Bricember early winter

A Note on Magic in the North-lands

Safe Magic

Civilized people in the North-lands use a gentle energy magic that is practical, but not flamboyant. It requires study and practice to achieve real skill.

Silmarish practitioners are called keyholders. Most are content to incline sick people toward health, to nudge crops into lush growth, and to adjust the worst storms into heavy downpours.

It's rare to heal someone near death, to grow fruit trees in non-arable land, or to disperse a hurricane. Even among the elite, such unusual feats are possible only if the underlying structures (the radices and the arcs) permit small repairs or adjustments to achieve spectacular results.

Practitioners merely help the natural processes along in a favorable direction. They do not change the energy configuration significantly. That would be *incantatio* or troll-magic, which is both dangerous and illegal.

Practitioners avoid large alterations to energy patterns. It's perilously easy to drift across the line separating the safe from the forbidden, when too much is attempted.

Perilous Magic

Troll-magic, or *incantatio*, is flamboyant, acute, and immediate in its effects. A troll-mage might pull a sick person back from the brink of death, grow watermelons in the desert, disperse a typhoon, or other such magnificent feats.

Unfortunately, it is the practice of troll-magic that turns humans into trolls.

It corrupts their bodies, starting with the ears and nose, which enlarge a little with each use of the power. It also unbalances their intellectual and emotional abilities.

A troll-witch who has practiced troll-magic for years will have a nose elongated like a curled thumb, ears the size of normal hands, swollen hands and feet, a severely curved spine, and much ill health. In his or her mind, insanity reigns.

Troll-magic is forbidden in all civilized places, because its use essentially creates powerful villains.

A few intellectual types use the terms *incantatio* and incantor or incantress. But most folk call this perilous practice troll-magic and its practitioners troll-mages or troll-witches. Nobody really wants to separate the idea of the magic from its effect: making trolls.

Insane trolls do crazy and hurtful things with their power. Newer trolls usually flock to older and more powerful trolls in the wild lands. They have no place in the civilized world. The authorities arrest them, because they cannot be left at large, and sentence them to death. (Incarceration is impractical. How do you imprison someone who can break any cell?)

Trolls don't live long, because the troll-disease, once started, progresses. When it progresses too far, the troll dies. Even potent trolls who elude capture live short lives.

Timeline for the North-lands Stories

ANCIENT TIMES

Skies of Navarys..................3000 years before *Troll-magic*

THE BRONZE AGE

Resonant Bronze ....2000 years before *Troll-magic*

BEFORE THE STEAM AGE

Rainbow's Lodestone.......... ~100 years before *Troll-magic*

Star-drake........... immediately after *Rainbow's Lodestone*

THE STEAM AGE

Sarvet's Wanderyar ....52 years before *Troll-magic*

Crossing the Naiad .. concurrent with *Sarvet's Wanderyar*

Livli's Gift ....38 years after *Sarvet's Wanderyar*
                          (14 years before *Troll-magic*)

Troll-magic ....the now of this timeline

The Troll's Belt .... contemporaneous with *Troll-magic*

Perilous Chance .... contemporaneous with *Troll-magic*

J.M. Ney-Grimm lives with her husband and children in Virginia, just east of the Blue Ridge Mountains. She's learning about permaculture gardening, post-carbon preparation, and debunking popular myths about food. The rest of the time she reads Robin McKinley and Lois McMaster Bujold, plays boardgames like Settlers of Catan, rears her twins, and writes stories set in her troll-infested North-lands.

Look for her novels and novellas at your favorite bookstore – online or on Main Street.

J.M. Ney-Grimm maintains a blog featuring flash fiction from her North-lands and other tidbits unearthed by her ever-active curiosity.

Visit her at JMNey-Grimm.com.